The
Littles
and the Great
Halloween Scare

Original title: *Tom Little's*
Great Halloween Scare

by **John Peterson**
Pictures by **Roberta Carter Clark**
Cover Illustrations by **Jacqueline Rogers**

A
LITTLE APPLE
PAPERBACK

SCHOLASTIC INC.
New York   Toronto   London   Auckland   Sydney

To my sisters
Mary Ann and Barbara

ISBN 0-590-42235-9

12 11 10 9 8 7 6 5 4 3 2 1   10   3 4 5 6 7 8/9

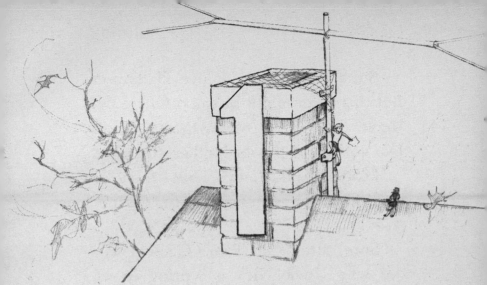

Lucy Little found her older brother, Tom, on the roof of the Biggs' house. He had just picked up the day's mail from the chimney mailbox.

"Tom!" Lucy said. She ran across the roof toward him. "You *promised* that today we'd think about something scary for Halloween! I've been looking all over for you."

"Hey — look at this." Tom waved a letter. "It's from Uncle Nick."

"There you go again, Tom. You aren't listening," Lucy said. "Don't you want to have fun on Halloween?"

"Sure!" said Tom. "I love Halloween. But this letter might be important, Lucy. Uncle Nick never writes to our family. I've got to get this to Mother and Dad."

"Okay," said Lucy. "But then we have to talk about Halloween. It's next week!"

"Sure, sure," said Tom. "Gee — I wonder why Uncle Nick is writing to us." The ten-year-old boy walked quickly across the rooftop. He pushed a loose shingle out of place. Under it was a hole into the attic of the house. Tom climbed through the hole. Eight-year-old Lucy climbed through after her brother.

Tom and Lucy were two of the three children of Mr. and Mrs. William T. Little. The Littles were tiny people. They were so tiny it was easy for Tom and Lucy to go through a hole the size of a roof shingle. Mr. Little, their father, was the tallest member of the family. He was exactly six inches tall.

The Littles looked just like ordinary people except for their smallness. And in one other way they were different. The Littles had tails. The tiny family didn't think it was strange that they had tails. They thought it was strange that big people *didn't* have tails. "They're born without them!" said Granny Little. "No one knows why."

The tiny Littles lived in a snug ten-room apartment. It was inside the walls of a house owned by Mr. George Bigg. Mr. and Mrs. Bigg and their son, Henry, had no idea that tiny people lived in the house with them.

Whenever the Biggs were near, the Littles stayed out of sight and tried not to make noise. This wasn't too hard for the Littles because the walls were thick enough to soften most noises. And there were passageways in the walls so the Littles could travel through the house without being seen.

Tiny people lived in many of the houses of the Big Valley. Sometimes the Littles visited with nearby tiny people and sometimes their friends visited them. But not often. It was a long way between houses. And the neighborhood outside the houses could be dangerous. There were cats and dogs and other animals and insects ready to pounce on anything small.

The Littles and their friends kept in touch mostly by airmail. The letters were delivered by glider. Cousin Dinky Little piloted the tiny airship. His wife, Della, often flew with him. When the wind was blowing in the right direction there were as many as two mail deliveries in a week.

Tom and Lucy liked to watch the mail come in. The blue and white glider zoomed in low over the house and dropped the mail into the chimney. Mr. Little and Uncle Pete (another member of the family) had stretched a fine net over the chimney hole. The net caught the letters, but it did not keep the smoke from rising.

Before Tom Little gave the letter from Uncle Nick to his father, he sniffed it. "I like the smell of the mail when the Biggs are using the fireplace," he said. "Especially when they are burning applewood."

"Look here, everyone!" Mr. Little held up the letter. "News from Uncle Nick."

"It must be a mistake," said Granny Little. She was sitting in her rocking chair near the fireplace. "Nick never writes."

Uncle Pete was holding baby Betsy, the youngest Little. His eyes opened wide. "My brother wrote a *letter*?" he said.

Mrs. Little came into the room holding a diaper. She took Betsy from Uncle Pete. Uncle Pete hopped out of his chair and rushed over to Mr. Little. "What does the old soldier say?" he asked.

Mr. Little squinted at the page. He

handed it to Uncle Pete. "What do you make of it?" he asked.

This is what it said:

DATE: 24 OCT
TIME: 1300 HRS
FROM: Major Nicholas Q. Little
32805315
STATION: Refuse Disposal Plant,
Big Valley Div
ATTENTION: William T. Little & Fam
REGARDING: Retirement fr Mouse
Force Brigade
PROCEDURE: Retirement w honors &
distinction of above named
effective 1600 hrs 26 Oct Will
proceed directly yr establishment
w intention to take up perm
residence among you Will arr
0900 hrs 29 Oct

regards NQL

Uncle Pete looked puzzled. "Er . . . I *think* it means that Uncle Nick is retiring from the army at the town dump and is coming to live with us at nine o'clock in the morning on October the 29th," he said.

Tom looked at the letter. He tried to read it, then gave up. "Well, why doesn't he say so?" he asked.

"Oh, you'd have to know Nick," Uncle Pete said. "That gobble-de-gook is army talk."

"Which one of my uncles *is* Uncle Nick?" asked Lucy. "Do I know him?"

"He's Uncle Pete's older brother," Mrs. Little told her. "You never met him, Lucy. He's been in the Mouse Brigade Army for years and years."

"Yes," said Uncle Pete. "Ever since the horrible Mouse Invasion of '35. A nasty bunch of mice attacked us right here." Uncle Pete pointed to the door. "My younger brother Tim lost his life that terrible day. But the rest of us managed to drive the mice away."

Granny Little shook her head. "Poor Nick! He was the oldest, but he was terribly afraid of mice."

"So am I," said Lucy. She shuddered.

"Oh dear — do we have to talk about mice?" asked Mrs. Little. She was rocking the baby in her arms.

"I'm not absolutely sure," Granny Little went on, "but I think he was hiding somewhere when Tim got killed."

"He never forgave himself for not being there," said Uncle Pete. "I suppose he wanted to do something to make up for it. Then one day he heard about the Trash Tinies."

"An amazing people!" said Mr. Little.

"*Who* are the Trash Tinies?" Lucy asked. "No one ever tells me anything!"

"They are tiny people who live in a hidden place in the town dump," Mr. Little said.

"Yuk!" said Lucy.

"Trash Tinies are completely surrounded by mice at all times," said Mr. Little. "It's a hard life."

"Nick decided to join the Mouse Force Brigade," Uncle Pete said, "and dedicate his life to protecting the Trash Tinies. It was a very unselfish thing to do."

"Gosh!" said Tom. "Uncle Nick must be a great man. Was he ever wounded?"

"I believe he was," said Uncle Pete.

Granny Little shook her head. "He never wrote a letter home in thirty years," she said. "Imagine that — thirty years! Wait'll I see him!"

"He must have been awfully busy," Tom said.

"A boy should write to his mother," said Granny Little. Then she smiled. "He was such a sweet child," she said. She looked up at Uncle Pete. "Let me see that letter."

Uncle Pete handed Granny Little the letter. She adjusted her glasses and looked at it. "Well," she said, "I suppose I was lucky he never wrote before this. They must speak a foreign language over at the town dump!"

Later that morning Lucy went looking for Tom again. He had *promised* to help her think up something scary for Halloween — but he kept disappearing.

Lucy finally found Tom in his room. At first he didn't see her. He was standing in front of his mirror waving a toothpick and saying, "Take that! And that . . . you mouse! !" Tom was pretending the toothpick was a sword.

"Tom!" yelled Lucy. "You stop playing! We have something important to do."

"I'm not *playing*," Tom said. "I'm practicing swordsmanship." Then he said, "Do you think Uncle Nick will teach me how to use a real needle sword?"

"Oh, Tom," said Lucy. "You already know how to use a sword. Uncle Pete taught you."

"That's different," Tom said. "Uncle Pete isn't a real soldier."

"Uncle Pete was in the Mouse Invasion of '35," Lucy said. "He fought the mice."

"I know that," said Tom, "but that was a long time ago." He drew the toothpick sword from his belt and lunged at the mirror. "Uncle Nick has been in the Mouse Force Brigade for *thirty* years. He must know *all* about fighting mice." He stuck the toothpick sword back in his belt. "I wish I could be a soldier like Uncle Nick."

"Hey, Tom!" said Lucy. "Why don't we dress up like soldiers for Halloween?"

Tom grinned. "That's just what I was

thinking," he said. "Uncle Nick would love it, wouldn't he?"

"It's not very scary though," Lucy said.

Tom pulled the toothpick sword from his belt again. "Come on, Lucy," he said in a low voice. "We'll sneak up on our enemies and find out their secrets." He slunk out of the room.

"What enemies?" Lucy followed Tom out of the room.

Tom put a finger to his lips. "Shh! Do you want them to hear us?" He tip-toed toward the kitchen. Lucy followed. They heard voices. They got as close to the kitchen as they could without being seen.

Uncle Pete was talking. ". . . and it looks just like a real battle," he finished.

"Henry made it all by himself?" It was Mrs. Little.

Tom whispered to Lucy, "They're talking about Henry Bigg."

Lucy nodded. "Is he our enemy?" she asked.

"Shhh!" said Tom. "Listen."

". . . had a lot of help from his father," said Uncle Pete.

"George Bigg is very good with his hands," Mrs. Little said.

"Speak up, Peter!" It was Granny Little. "What did Mr. Bigg make?" The old lady leaned forward in her chair. Her hand cupped her ear.

"A diorama," said Uncle Pete. "Henry Bigg made a diorama for school. His father helped him."

"A dio — what?"

"A diorama," repeated Uncle Pete. "It's a scene of the Civil War inside a box. Soldiers from the North are fighting to take a bridge from some Southern soldiers. He has toy soldiers in it and puffs of cotton that look like smoke from gun shots — things like that. It's quite real looking."

"Oh," said Granny Little. "I *hate* war."

"Everybody hates war, Granny," said Uncle Pete.

Outside the room, Tom whispered to Lucy, "We've got to see that. Where is it?"

"It's in the Biggs' kitchen, right on the counter," Lucy said. "Anyway, it was. Maybe Henry has taken it to school."

"Let's go see," said Tom. "We might get some good ideas for our costumes." Tom had been crouching down on one knee listening. He started to stand up.

Lucy pulled him down. "Wait! Now they're talking about *us*!" she said.

"The poor dears always think they scare us on Halloween," Mrs. Little was saying. "It's so cute."

"I wonder what they'll do this year," said Granny Little.

Uncle Pete laughed. "I always have to

try so hard to keep from busting out laughing," he said.

Granny Little chuckled. "They're so cute," she said.

Tom signaled for Lucy to be quiet and follow him. They tip-toed to a back room in the apartment. They went out a door leading to the wall passageway. As soon as they were out of ear-shot, Tom exploded. "Boy—they think we're *cute!*"

"Golly," Lucy said. "I always thought we were really scaring them."

"OK, OK," Tom said. "So they've never been scared, eh?" His eyes narrowed. "This year, Lucy, we're *really* going to scare them!"

"What are we going to do, Tom?" asked Lucy.

"I don't know," Tom said. "But it'll be the biggest scare this family ever had, you can be sure of that."

Tom and Lucy wanted to get a close look at Henry Bigg's diorama. They took the tin-can elevator down to the Biggs' kitchen. The elevator was an old soup can. The Littles had rigged up some pieces of string and some pulleys to operate it. The elevator went between the walls of the house.

The children hopped out of the tin-can elevator and ran to the kitchen wall. They stood behind an electric socket that was over the kitchen counter. Tom looked through the socket holes. "All clear!" he said.

"Henry's in school. Mr. Bigg is working. And Mrs. Bigg won't be back until three o'clock," Lucy said. "I heard her say so."

The Biggs didn't know it, but their electric socket on the kitchen counter was also a secret door. The Littles used the socket door once or twice a day. When the coast was clear they would dash through the door and grab the best leftovers from the Biggs' meals.

Mrs. Little had never bothered to learn how to cook. Mrs. Bigg was such a good cook it wasn't necessary. And, of course, the Biggs never noticed that any food was missing. The Littles took only a few scraps at a time. As far as the Littles were concerned that was always more than enough. They could feed their whole family and any number of guests that might be visiting them.

Tom pushed open the secret socket door. He and Lucy ran across the counter to Henry's diorama.

Tom stopped just outside the diorama. "Wow!" he said. "This is terrific!"

"Oh, Tom," Lucy said. "It looks so real."

She entered the diorama. Tom was right behind her. They walked softly, looking to the right and left. The plastic Civil War soldiers were a little taller than the children. Suddenly Tom drew his toothpick sword from his belt. He raised it over his head. "Come on, Lucy!" he yelled. "Let's help these guys capture the bridge." He ran forward.

Lucy ran after Tom. When she got to the bridge Tom was laughing. "It was easy," he said. "I captured the bridge all by myself. These guys never moved."

Lucy looked around. "Oh, Tom," she said. "Wasn't it terrible? Men from our country fighting and killing each other."

"Yeah, it was crazy," Tom said. "But I guess there wasn't any other way to keep the country *united*. Anyway, that's what I read in Henry's history book."

"I wish we could vote when we grow up," said Lucy.

Tom laughed. "Wow, Lucy," he said. "You sure can *wish*! Big people would never let us vote."

"That's because big people don't even know that we tiny people *exist*!" Lucy said. "If they knew we were here — and that we are real people — and that we care about our country too, maybe they would let us vote."

"Lucy," said Tom seriously. "The worst thing that could happen would be for the big people to know about us."

"I know." Lucy looked down from the bridge at the painted water below. "Usually it doesn't bother me. But all of a sudden it seems like the saddest thing that we know all about Henry and he doesn't know anything about us."

"It is kind of strange in a way," Tom said. "But that's the way it is."

Just then the kitchen door flew open. Henry Bigg walked into the room. Tom and Lucy barely had time to leap off the bridge and hide beneath it.

Henry walked straight to the diorama where Tom and Lucy were hiding. He leaned over the counter. He was looking right at the battle scene. "Bang, bang," he said softly.

Tom and Lucy huddled together under the bridge. "Tom!" whispered Lucy. "What'll we . . ."

"Sh!" Tom said.

Henry opened one of the cabinets above the kitchen counter. He took out a jar of peanut butter. He opened a drawer and got out a loaf of bread.

Tom and Lucy could see Henry through the floor boards of the bridge.

The big boy spread the peanut butter on a slice of bread. He opened the refrigerator and poured a glass of milk.

Henry ate the sandwich and drank the milk. He kept looking at the diorama.

Tom whispered as quietly as he could into Lucy's ear. "He's home for lunch. I wonder why. He doesn't come home for lunch when Mrs. Bigg isn't here."

Henry took a Civil War figure from his pocket. He placed it on the bridge in the diorama. It was right over Tom's and Lucy's heads.

Henry got his head down close to one of the figures attacking the bridge. He squinted. "You got a bead on 'em," he said. "Shoot!" Then, "Bang!" With one finger Henry knocked the soldier on the bridge into the painted water. He lay right next to the Little children.

Tom sucked in his breath. He gripped Lucy's arm.

"He'll go to school in a minute," Tom whispered. "Then we'll get out of here."

Just then Henry picked up the diorama!

Tom and Lucy hung on to the struts of the bridge to keep from rolling around.

Henry started for the door!

"Tom!" whispered Lucy. "He's going to school!"

Henry opened the outside door and went out onto the porch.

Suddenly he spun around and walked back into the house. He placed the diorama on the kitchen table. He walked into the bathroom and closed the door.

"Come on, Lucy!" said Tom. They both jumped to their feet and ran from the diorama to the table.

"How'll we get off the table?" asked Lucy.

"No time!" Tom said. "Quick! In here." He pointed to a hollowed out pumpkin that was in the center of the table. The children climbed through the mouth of the pumpkin face. They were just in time. They looked through the pumpkin's eyes and saw Henry come out of the bathroom.

The big boy picked up the diorama. "I'm not going to forget you this time," he said aloud. He went out the kitchen door.

"Whew! What luck!" Tom said. "Good thing Henry went to the bathroom or we'd be on the way to school."

Lucy was laughing now that it was over. "Gee, maybe we should have gone," she said.

"Henry's school is *four* blocks away," Tom said. "Do you know how long it would take us to get back from there?"

Lucy was still laughing in a silly way. "We could ride back in Henry's pocket," she said.

"Sure, sure," Tom said. "On the second Tuesday of next week."

The day finally came when Uncle Nick was expected. The letter hadn't said whether he was coming by land or by air — whether he would walk or come in a glider. The Littles decided the best place to wait was on the Biggs' roof. They could watch the sky and the ground at the same time.

All of the Littles were on the roof that morning. They wanted to give Uncle Nick a big welcome. It was an important day in his life.

Even Granny Little made the trip up to the roof. "It's a glorious day!" she said breathing deeply.

Mrs. Little held baby Betsy close. She looked over the tree-tops and the houses. "Uncle Nick will love it here," she said. "It's so beautiful and peaceful — nothing at all like the *dump,* I'm sure."

"I'll bet he has some fantastic stories to tell," Uncle Pete said.

"Keep your eyes on the yard, Tom," said Mr. Little. "We don't want to miss him."

Tom leaned over the edge of the roof. "I'm looking," he said. "What about Lucy? Can't she help?"

"I am!" shouted Lucy. She stood near the chimney. "I'm watching the sky just like Daddy said." The tiny girl shaded her eyes and searched above the trees.

After a while it was past the time when Uncle Nick was supposed to get there. No one had seen any sign of him.

"That's very strange," Uncle Pete said. "Nick was always on time for everything! In fact, he used to be *ahead* of time. He called it Mouse Force Time — said all

Mouse Force men were ten minutes ahead of everyone."

"Something must have happened," said Mr. Little.

"He would have sent another message if he couldn't make it," said Uncle Pete.

"Oh dear," Mrs. Little said. "I hope he's all right."

Finally — an hour later — the Littles gave up and went back to the apartment inside the walls of the Biggs' house.

"Hold everything!" Uncle Pete said as he opened the door. "Something's wrong!"

The Littles rushed into the room.

"What's the matter?" asked Mr. Little.

"I don't know exactly," said Uncle Pete, "but the place looks different somehow."

"It's neater," said Granny Little.

"*Neater?*" said Mr. Little and Uncle Pete at the same time.

"It *is* neater," Mrs. Little said. "I left

some of Betsy's toys on the sofa. They've been picked up."

Mr. Little pulled a chest out from under the sofa. "Something else is wrong," he said. "Look at this weapons chest."

The Littles ran to the opened chest. It was empty.

"Everything's gone!" Tom said. "ALL the bows and arrows."

"What in blue blazes is going on here?" said Uncle Pete.

"I CAN ANSWER THAT!" boomed a slow deep voice from the next room.

The door opened. A short man in a

brown uniform walked into the room. His chest was covered with medals.

"Nick!" said Granny Little. "So there you are!"

"And just in time too," Uncle Pete said. He limped over and shook his brother's hand and patted him on the back. "We've got a problem. Someone has stolen all of our weapons. We are totally defenseless!"

"Exactly!" Uncle Nick said. "And now — may I ask — what do you plan to do when the mice attack?"

"Mice?" Uncle Pete said. "Where?"

"Nick!" said Granny Little. "*You* took the weapons!"

"Exactly!" said Uncle Nick. "They're safe in the kitchen."

"And did you tidy up the living room?" asked Mrs. Little.

"Exactly!" Uncle Nick said. "An old military habit. A place for everything and everything in its place."

"Nick, you old rascal!" said Uncle Pete. He looked sideways at his brother. "What is this game you're playing?"

"No game," said Uncle Nick. "I wanted you to see for yourselves how easy it would be for an enemy to sneak up on you, get into your apartment without being seen, and take all your weapons."

The Littles looked at each other puzzled.

"Ah ha!" Uncle Pete said suddenly. He used his cane to walk back and forth in front of the fireplace. "You outflanked us. Brilliant!"

"He out-*what* us?" said Granny Little.

"A classic war movement, Granny," said Uncle Pete. "We were all up on the roof — leaving no one to guard the place. Somehow Nick sneaked by us, captured the place single-handedly, and disarmed us." He smiled.

"That's more or less it," Uncle Nick agreed. "I hope you have all learned something from my little performance."

"You scared us all out of our wits," Granny Little said. "That's all I got out of it."

Lucy ran to the kitchen door. "I'll get the bows and arrows," she said.

The tiny girl opened the door and screamed.

Mr. Little and Tom rushed to Lucy's side.

"Stop!" Tom yelled.

A great white mouse was crouching on the kitchen floor.

"BACK, MUS MUS!" shouted Uncle Nick in his deep voice. He walked toward the kitchen.

The mouse backed into the corner of the room.

"Great ghosts!" Uncle Pete said. "You brought a *mouse* with you!"

Lucy ran to her mother in tears.

"Meet Mus Mus," said Uncle Nick. "He won't hurt you, Lucy. He's a white house mouse." As Uncle Nick came up to him, the mouse rolled over on its back, its paws in the air. Uncle Nick patted the animal on the tummy.

The Littles crowded up to the kitchen door.

"Is it safe?" Mr. Little asked.

"I can't look," said Lucy. She clung to her mother and kept her eyes tightly closed.

"Why do you want a mouse?" asked Uncle Pete. "Do you really need to own a mouse?" He shook his head.

"Mus Mus does exactly what I tell him to do," Uncle Nick said. "Don't you, old fellow?" The mouse rolled over and looked at the major. He stroked the animal's back. "I use him to track down the ordinary house mouse."

"There are no mice around this house," said Mr. Little. "George Bigg wouldn't stand for it."

"Well I declare!" said Granny Little after she had got her glasses up on her nose and saw the mouse. "I wouldn't believe it if I didn't see it with these old eyes. Why Nick, you were always scared to death of mice."

"I was?" Uncle Nick said. "I don't remember that."

"Well, look at him now!" said Uncle Pete. "He looks like a regular mouse tamer."

"Gee," said Tom quietly. "That mouse is almost beautiful . . . in a way."

"And he's as tame as a pussycat," said Uncle Nick. "Watch this!" The tiny major spoke sharply. "Roll over, Mus Mus!"

The white mouse immediately rolled over. He went from one side of the kitchen floor to the other.

"My goodness!" Mrs. Little said. "Watch out for the shelves."

"Sit up, Mus Mus!" commanded Uncle Nick.

The mouse sat up on its hind legs.

"Wow!" Tom said. "That's really keen."

"Now *that's* a mouse!" said Uncle Pete. "He's marvelous."

Mrs. Little spoke quietly. "Uncle Nick," she said, "you are welcome to live with us for as long as you like. But . . . but — and I hope you understand I don't want to hurt your feelings—"

Mr. Little broke in, "I think my wife is trying to say she would rather not have mice in the apartment," he said. "That is, if you were thinking of keeping him here." He turned to Mrs. Little. "Is that right, dear?"

Mrs. Little nodded.

"I don't blame you," Uncle Nick said. "I don't blame you at all for feeling that way. I hate the brutes myself. I've spent a lifetime fighting them."

"Oh, I'm so glad you agree," Mrs. Little said.

"But, of course Mus Mus is not a plain ordinary mouse," Uncle Nick went on. "He comes from a very important strain of mice — very important indeed! I found out all about him in a book called *The Field Guide to North American Mammals*. It was thrown away in the dump. His real name is *Mus Musculus*." The major looked around at all the Littles. "That's *Latin*," he said proudly. "I shortened it to Mus Mus."

"It's a cute name," Lucy said.

"Then I realized that Mus Mus might actually have been in the same room with the *President of the United States,*" said Uncle Nick.

"You don't say!" Uncle Pete said.

"Yessiree!" said Uncle Nick. "The book said he wasn't your ordinary house mouse at all. He was a White House mouse."

"Yes, yes — go on," Uncle Pete said.

"Why, I just told you," said Uncle Nick. "He's a *White House* mouse. He comes from the White House . . . in Washington, D.C. How do you like that for a mouse?"

"But, Uncle Nick," said Tom. "That means . . .

"*How* interesting!" Mr. Little broke in. "That is certainly the most remarkable mouse we have ever seen." He looked over at Mrs. Little and shrugged his shoulders.

The next morning Uncle Nick was up before all the other Littles. He was writing at the kitchen table when everyone came in to breakfast.

"I say — Nick!" said Uncle Pete. "Let's get these papers off the table, old man. We've got to have our breakfast."

"What? What?" said Uncle Nick. He didn't look up.

"Will and Tom have gone to get some breakfast leftovers," Uncle Pete said. "You are taking up all the room at the kitchen table."

Uncle Nick kept right on writing. He waved a hand at Uncle Pete. "By all means," he said. "Have breakfast. I'm not hungry myself."

Mrs. Little whispered to Uncle Pete. "Don't bother him," she said. "We can eat in the dining room."

Mr. Little and Tom returned with the leftovers. "We're in luck," said Mr. Little. "Here's a quarter of a pancake."

"I'll heat the leftover coffee," Granny Little said.

Uncle Nick stopped writing. He looked up at Granny Little. "Granny," he said, "can you keep the noise down for just a moment, please?" He looked thoughtfully at the ceiling. "I'm in the middle of an idea." The major chewed on his pencil for a moment. He began writing again.

"Umph!" snorted Granny Little. "I didn't know you were a writer." She turned her back on Uncle Nick and mumbled, "A person would think you could have written a letter home once or twice in thirty years."

"What's Uncle Nick writing?" asked Tom.

Uncle Pete sneaked a look over his brother's shoulder. He raised his eyebrows and nodded his head slowly. When he joined the others in the dining room, he said, "Looks as though Nick is writing the story of his life. He calls it *Nick Little Battles the Savage Mice.*"

"Gee!" Tom said. "What a title."

"I don't care for it," Mrs. Little said. "It's too violent."

Uncle Pete frowned at Mrs. Little. "You can't make an omelette without breaking eggs," he said.

"I never make omelettes," said Mrs. Little. "I don't cook at all. You know that."

"Uncle Pete was trying to explain," Mr. Little said, "that you can't protect Trash Tinies without fighting mice."

"Oh?" said Mrs. Little. "Well, anyway — if Uncle Nick can't write a nice book I don't see why he bothers."

"Golly, Mother," said Tom. "How do we know it's not nice? It's about Uncle Nick's adventures."

"If it's about mice how could it be nice?" said Lucy.

Suddenly Uncle Nick came to the dining room door.

"Uncle Nick," said Tom. "Can I read your book? Can I?"

"*May I*, Tom," corrected Mrs. Little.

"May I, Uncle Nick?" asked Tom.

Uncle Nick laughed. "I've just started writing it," he said.

"Uncle Pete said you were wounded," Tom went on. "Were you wounded?"

Uncle Nick looked at the floor. "I . . . ah . . " he said. He shifted his feet. Then he looked quickly at the ceiling. "Yes, Tom . . . I was wounded. It was at the Battle of the Automobile Seat about ten years ago. There was this nest of mice in the seat and . . ."

"*Where* were you wounded, Uncle Nick?" interrupted Tom.

"Tom — don't interrupt your uncle," said Mrs. Little.

"Ah, it was," Uncle Nick finished quickly in a low voice, "in the *seat*. I was wounded in the seat of the automobile as we were closing in on the mice."

Uncle Nick turned and went back to the kitchen and began writing again.

"I meant where was he wounded on his body," said Tom. "Not where in the battle."

"I don't think Uncle Nick wants to talk about it," said Mr. Little.

"He's too modest," said Uncle Pete. "He's just too doggoned modest."

"What does *modest* mean?" Lucy asked.

"It means that Uncle Pete thinks your Uncle Nick doesn't want to boast about all the things he's done," said Mr. Little.

"He *doesn't*?" said Tom. "Golly! I want to hear all about Uncle Nick's adventures. If I'd done what he's done I'd tell everybody!"

After breakfast Tom and Lucy took Mus Mus for a walk on a leash. "Uncle Nick says he needs the exercise," said Tom.

"Tom — you haven't thought about Halloween at all," Lucy said. "You promised to think of a good scare idea."

"Oh, we have time for that, Lucy," said Tom. "I'll think of something soon." He ran with the mouse in the wall passageway.

"But we don't have any costumes," said Lucy running after them.

"Uncle Nick says he'll help me with my swordsmanship," Tom said. "Isn't that great?"

When they got back to the apartment, everyone was in the living room. Uncle Nick was standing by the fireplace talking. "I have a plan all worked out," he said.

"Why do we need a plan?" asked Granny Little. She looked around at everyone.

"Oh, Granny!" said Uncle Pete. "Just listen to Nick. He understands these things. It's about time we had a plan. We tiny people live a dangerous life. We should be ready for any emergency."

"We Littles have lived in this house since it was built," Granny Little said, "and we never had a plan of any kind." She shook her finger. "And we're still here. And in good health too."

Uncle Nick turned to Mrs. Little. "First," he said, "you really should learn how to cook."

"Oh dear," said Mrs. Little.

"Of course, that *will* take some time," said Uncle Nick. "In the meantime we'll just have to be mighty careful when we take food from the Biggs."

"We always were," Granny Little whispered to Mrs. Little. She patted her hand.

"Mrs. Bigg *is* a terrific cook," Uncle Pete said. "Have you thought of that, Nick?"

"Just remember," Uncle Nick said, "that every time we go near the Biggs there is a chance that we'll be seen. Someday it's bound to happen.

"Second," Uncle Nick went on, "we should have a practice alert every now and then."

"What do you mean?" asked Mr. Little.

"We should make believe that the Biggs have seen us," said Uncle Nick. "Then we'll leave the house as quickly as we can — using a plan of escape I have worked out."

Granny Little shook her head firmly. "*I'm* not leaving this house for make-believe!" she said.

Uncle Nick got out a large sheet of paper. He hung it on the wall. "This is a rough map of the Biggs' house and the surrounding land," he said. "If you look closely you will see that I have marked some of the danger areas in red and orange."

Tom squinted at the map. "What are the danger areas?" he asked.

"They are the places where we can expect the most trouble," said Uncle Nick. "Red stands for the points where mice can most easily get into the house. The orange areas are places where the Biggs are most likely to see us."

"I'm scared," said Lucy. She walked over and sat next to her mother. Mrs. Little was holding baby Betsy and humming softly.

"We must stay away from the orange areas," Uncle Nick said. "And we will place a twenty-four hour guard at the red areas."

"Hold on there, Nick!" called Uncle Pete. "What's this guard business?"

Uncle Nick got out another paper. "I have prepared a schedule," he said. "It's figured out so we all share the job of guard duty equally. Of course, Granny isn't on it. She's older and hard of hearing."

Granny Little snorted.

"Did you say *twenty-four* hours?" Uncle Pete asked.

"Exactly," said Uncle Nick.

"Well," Uncle Pete said, "does that mean at *night* too?"

"Exactly," said Uncle Nick.

"Let me see that list." Uncle Pete grabbed the paper from Uncle Nick's hand. He looked it over. Then he jabbed his finger at the paper. "That's *me*," he said, "from two in the morning until six on Tuesday — *every* Tuesday!"

Uncle Nick looked at the paper. "Exactly!" he said. "And on Fridays too."

"Nick," said Uncle Pete slowly and with great force, "what's all this poppy-cock about guard duty anyway?"

"Twenty-four hour guard duty is imperative," Uncle Nick said.

"Well, if you want to stand guard, go ahead." Uncle Pete limped to the door. "As for me, I need my sleep." And he opened the door and walked out.

"It sure is strange," said Lucy to Tom.

They were in the Biggs' attic. The day was gloomy. The attic was darker than usual.

"What's strange?" Tom asked.

"The closer we get to Halloween, the more scary the attic is," said Lucy.

Tom was leading the way. They were crawling over boxes, trunks, and old furniture. The darkest corner of the attic lay ahead.

"Gee, Lucy — it's the *same* old attic whether it's Halloween or not," Tom said.

"I still think it's scarier," said Lucy.

"The Biggs have piled a lot of stuff in this corner," Tom said, "but I know that some of Henry's GI Joe clothes are here someplace. They might make good Halloween costumes."

"Are we just going to take them?" Lucy asked.

"We'll bring them back right after Halloween," said Tom. "Henry still wants them. I heard him say so."

"Tom — I'm sorry for Uncle Nick," said Lucy. "Aren't you?"

Tom stopped. He sat down to rest on the toe of a shoe. He scratched his head. "Nobody wants to do the things that Uncle Nick thinks we should do," he said. "But I'd *like* to do guard duty."

"At night?"

"It would be fun," said Tom, his face lighting up. "Maybe I'd see a mouse."

"We haven't seen any mice since that time the Biggs went on vacation," said Lucy, "and those sloppy people came to live here while they were gone. Remember?"

"And we'll *never* have any the way Mrs. Bigg keeps such a clean house," Tom said.

"I *hate* mice, Tom!"

"Me too," Tom said. "But wouldn't it be terrific if we had some . . . just for Uncle Nick?"

At last they were in the darkest corner of the attic. "I'll look over this way," Tom said. "You look through that box."

Tom searched for a few moments. Suddenly he heard Lucy yell.

The tiny boy rushed toward the sound of Lucy's voice. He raced around a cardboard box.

There was Lucy. She was thrashing around on the floor. "ICK!" she yelled. "Get these cobwebs off me! It's in my hair and everything."

Tom ran toward Lucy.

Then he saw the spider. It was rushing down the web toward the tiny girl.

Out of the corner of his eye Tom saw
a safety pin. Luckily it was open. Tom
scooped up the pin on the run. He dived
at the spider.

Lucy ducked. Tom speared the spider
with the safety pin.

The spider rolled off the web to the
floor.

"Tom! You killed a spider!" Lucy sat
up. She forgot about the cobwebs for
the moment.

"I got it just in time," Tom said.

"Oh Tom — you never should have,"
said Lucy with tears in her eyes. "It was
just coming to see what broke its web,
that's all. Spiders are wonderful crea-
tures. You shouldn't kill them."

"Are you nuts, Lucy?" yelled Tom. "It
was coming right for you. You were
yelling."

"That's because spider webs are icky when they get all over you," Lucy said. She went back to pulling the cobwebs from her face and hair and clothes.

"Wow — a lot of thanks I get for helping you," Tom said.

"But Tom — you *know* that spiders catch bad insects. You know that!"

"Forget it, Lucy!" said Tom. "Just forget it, will you?" He spun around and walked away. "Let's get out of here."

Lucy ran after Tom. "What about the Halloween costumes?" she yelled.

"I don't feel like looking anymore," Tom said. He kept walking.

Lucy ran her fingers through her hair. "Tom — wait!" she said. "I can't get this stuff off me."

When they got to the tin-can elevator, Lucy said, "Hey, Tom — let's take a swim. I can clean off these cobwebs easy that way."

The children climbed into the tin can. They started down. "Aw, come on, Tom," said Lucy. "Let's have some fun. The Biggs aren't home. Wouldn't you like to go swimming?"

A few moments later Tom was floating on his back in the Biggs' goldfish bowl in the living room. Lucy was sitting on the edge of the bowl dangling her feet in the water.

"How can we get a scary idea for Halloween now?" Lucy said. "It's too late, isn't it? Halloween is tonight and we don't have any costumes or any good ideas. Darn it, Tom! It's all your fault."

"Quiet, I'm thinking," Tom said. "I got some ideas, but nothing is scary enough. We have to really scare them this time so we'll know for sure they're not pretending."

"Hey, Tom — how about . . ."

"Shhh!" said Tom. "I'm thinking."

It was Halloween eve. The Littles were alone in the Biggs' house. Mr. and Mrs. Bigg were at a movie. And Henry was spending the night at a friend's house.

Mrs. Little was putting Betsy to bed. Uncle Nick was out patrolling the passageways with Mus Mus. The rest of the Littles were talking in the kitchen.

"I don't really think that Nick is annoyed with us," said Uncle Pete.

"I'm not so sure," said Mr. Little. "He's out there right now doing the guard duty he wants us all to do."

"He thinks it's important," Tom said, "even if we don't."

"I suppose it's hard for him to retire after all those years," Mr. Little said.

Granny Little nodded. "It's too bad there aren't some real mice in the house," she said. "He's so active. It would give the poor boy something to do."

The Biggs' front doorbell rang. It rang so loud in the house that the Littles could hear it faintly through the walls. It had been ringing all evening.

Uncle Pete laughed. "Those trick-or-treaters again," he said. "They never give up even when nobody's home."

"I wish we could go trick-or-treating," Lucy said. "I'll bet it's fun."

"Trick-or-treating is fun for the big children," said Mr. Little, "but it would never work for tiny children. The other tiny families are too far away for that."

"We have a nice Halloween tradition," said Uncle Pete. "It's fun to try and scare your parents. When I was a boy we thought Halloween was the most fun of any holiday."

Uncle Pete turned and winked at Mr. Little. "I wonder what scary thing these two will come up with this year," he went on. "Last year they scared us all out of our wits, remember?"

"We haven't . . ." began Lucy.

"You'll never know until it happens, Uncle Pete," said Tom.

Mrs. Little came into the room. "The Biggs left the radio on," she said.

"Good!" said Uncle Pete. "I'd like to listen for a while. It'll calm me down before Tom and Lucy's big scare." He stood up. "What kind of music is it? Not that terrible kid stuff I hope."

"It's not music," Mrs. Little said. "Some people are talking about one of those big battles — World War II, I think — or was it the Civil War? Anyway, one of them wrote a book about it."

"Oh good," Uncle Pete said. He

yawned. "Just what I need to perk me up. Hope Nick gets back soon. He'd like that."

"I left the cork out of the wall," said Mrs. Little. "I thought you might want to listen."

The "cork" that Mrs. Little was talking about was usually stuck in a hole in the Littles' living room wall. Their wall was the same wall that faced the Biggs' living room. The hole was about the size of a quarter. On the Biggs' side the hole was covered with wallpaper, so the Biggs didn't know it was there. Mr. Little had punched many tiny holes in the wallpaper with one of Mrs. Bigg's sewing needles.

Whenever the Biggs' radio was playing it could be heard through the tiny holes as long as the cork was out. Voices were coming into the Littles' living room as Uncle Pete sat down in his favorite chair. He leaned forward and listened.

"Lucy!" Tom whispered. "I've got it. I've got the idea!"

"Oh Tom!"

"Go to your bedroom," Tom said. "Then sneak out into the wall passageway. Don't let anybody see you go. I'll meet you there."

In a few moments the children were out of the apartment.

"What's the idea?" asked Lucy. "Tell me."

"Quick!" said Tom. "We don't have much time." He ran to the tin-can elevator. Lucy followed.

The elevator got to the ground floor. Tom ran ahead to the Biggs' living room.

"We have to do it before Uncle Pete stops listening to the radio," Tom said. "Hurry, Lucy."

"Do what, Tom?"

They went through a secret door that was under the living room radiator. Tom began climbing an electric cord near the bookshelves.

"Wait, Tom," called Lucy. "I'm out of breath."

The electric cord was attached to a radio-phonograph tape-recorder on one of the shelves.

Tom stood in front of the machine. The dials glowed. "I know how to work this thing," he said. "I've watched Henry do it."

Lucy pulled herself up onto the shelf. "Tom, *please* tell me what we're doing." she asked.

"Terrific!" said Tom. "They left the microphone plugged in." He turned to Lucy. "We're going to scare the daylights out of Uncle Pete, that's what!"

"How?"

"We're going to interrupt the radio broadcast with a special announcement," Tom said.

"We are?" said Lucy. "How?"

"See this lever?" said Tom pointing. "Where it says 'selector'?"

"Yes."

"When I signal you," said Tom, "push the lever from 'radio' to 'mike' — OK?"

"What are you going to say?" Lucy asked.

"Just listen," said Tom. He looked at dials and buttons and levers on the machine. "Wait — this red button. It's supposed to be pushed in . . . I think. Oh, it is in. I think that's right."

"Tom, how can you tell?" Lucy said. "It looks so complicated."

"OK — wait'll I get to the microphone," said Tom. The boy ran to the other side of the shelf. He turned and waved at

Lucy. Tom waited a few seconds, then, in a deep voice he said, **"We interrupt this program for a special announcement!"**

Lucy jumped into the air when she heard her brother's voice booming out of the loudspeakers.

Tom went on, **"Tiny People — some of them only four inches tall — have been discovered in the walls of many houses in the Big Valley."**

Lucy clapped a hand over her mouth.

"There is no reason to be alarmed," said Tom. **"They can't hurt you. They're too small and they only have bows and arrows, spears and swords."** Tom was trying to keep from laughing. **"If you think you may have tiny people in the walls of your home, call this special number — 887-4043. Special tiny people removers will be sent to your house to investigate."** Tom looked over at Lucy. She was down on her knees holding her sides and laughing.

Tom went on, **"We said the tiny people couldn't hurt you, but there is one thing**

to watch out for. Be sure not to pick up the tiny people — they may bite!"

Tom began to giggle. He held his hand over his mouth. Finally he calmed down enough to say, **"Keep tuned to this station for more news of tiny people."**

Tom ran over to the 'selector' lever and pushed it to 'radio.' The regular program came from the loudspeakers again.

"Oh Tom!" gasped Lucy. "That was so funny."

"So Uncle Pete thought we couldn't scare him," Tom said. "Ha! I'll bet he jumped two inches when he heard that."

"What if everybody believed you, Tom?" asked Lucy.

Tom was still laughing. "They'd *better* believe," he said, "or they wouldn't be scared."

"But what will they do?" said Lucy.

Tom stopped smiling suddenly. "We'd better get back there," he said. He ran for the electric cord.

Tom and Lucy rushed into the apartment.

Uncle Nick was standing in the middle of the room. The rest of the Littles were running in and out of the room carrying things. Uncle Nick was reading from a paper. ". . . only your toothbrush and a change of clothing. Don't waste time. Be sure to get a weapon from the weapons chest. Peter — you get a canteen of water . . ."

"Oh! Here are Tom and Lucy," said Mrs. Little. "Thank goodness!"

"What's going on?" Tom asked.

"We've been discovered," said Mr. Little, speaking quickly. "We have to get out of the house before they come after us."

"No need to panic," Uncle Nick said. "Just work quickly, and don't forget anything that is on my list. Any questions?"

Lucy looked at Tom.

"Wait a minute, everyone," said Tom. "Lucy and I . . ."

"No time for talk, Tom," said Uncle Nick. "We'll explain later what happened. You and Lucy go to your rooms and pack a bag. Take only your toothbrush and one change of clothing."

"But . . ." Tom said.

Just then Mrs. Little came running in from the living room. "The Biggs are home!" she whispered.

Everyone ran into the living room and up to the hole in the wall.

"Dad," Tom began.

"Quiet, son," said Mr. Little. "Let's find out if they have heard the news."

"It's all a mis . . ." Tom began again.

"Shhh!" said Nick fiercely

Mr. Bigg's voice came through the hole. "I've seen better movies," he said. "He's not *my* favorite actor."

"I loved it," said Mrs. Bigg.

Back in the Littles' apartment Mr. Little looked at the others. "Good! They haven't heard," he whispered.

Mr. Bigg's voice boomed into the room. "Umph! Well, anyway — I went with you like you asked. Good thing I had the brains to tape that Civil War talk show while we were out. Now I can sit down and listen to it in peace." He laughed. "I won't have missed a thing, thanks to this tape recorder."

"Oh, oh!" whispered Mr. Little. "*Now* they'll be getting the news. Darn it! I wondered why they left the radio on."

Tom grabbed the cork and stuffed it into the hole.

"Tom — what are you doing?" said Mr. Little.

"Listen, everyone—please!" Tom said. "*I* did it! It was me you heard telling about the tiny people in the walls."

"What!" shouted Uncle Pete.

"It was a joke to scare you, Uncle Pete," Tom went on. "I switched from the radio to the microphone."

Lucy nodded. "It was Tom."

"A *joke*?" said Uncle Nick.

"It was our Halloween scare," said Tom. "But I didn't know Mr. Bigg had the tape recorder on! I didn't know that!"

"Oh dear!" said Mrs. Little.

"Tom! I'm surprised at you," said Mr. Little.

"We've got to stop Bigg from hearing that program," said Uncle Pete.

"You can't do that," said Mrs. Little.

"Let's go!" said Uncle Nick. He ran for the door.

"*Uncle Nick!*" screamed Lucy. She was pointing to the floor. "You lost your tail!"

Uncle Nick stopped running. He spun around.

All the Littles were staring at a tail on the floor.

The tiny major walked back and picked up the tail. "All right," he said. "Now you know where I was wounded. Darn mouse bit my tail right off." He shook the tail. "This one's a fake." Then he stuffed it into his pocket.

No one said anything.

Uncle Nick turned and headed for the door. "Tail or no tail," he said, "we have to stop that man from finding out about us."

Uncle Nick ran into the wall passageway. Mus Mus, the white mouse, was waiting. "Let's go, fellow!" commanded Uncle Nick.

Uncle Pete, Mr. Little, Tom, and Lucy were right behind them.

At the secret door to the Biggs' living room they stopped.

Uncle Nick pushed the door open slowly.

They heard voices.

"He's playing the tape of the program now," said Uncle Nick closing the door.

"How can *we* stop Mr. Bigg from listening?" asked Mr. Little.

"Do you know where the master electrical switch is?" asked Uncle Nick.

"Of course," Uncle Pete said. "We Littles are good electricians. We always have been. Why, we have solved and repaired many electrical problems from *inside* the walls." Uncle Pete laughed.

"Old Bigg doesn't even know it, but we've helped him many times."

"Yes, yes," said Uncle Nick impatiently. "Can you throw the switch?"

"We can do it," said Mr. Little.

"Then get going," said Uncle Nick. "Let's do *something*."

"Bigg'll just turn on the master switch again," said Uncle Pete.

"While he's doing it we will have some time," said Uncle Nick. "I'll think of something to stop him from hearing the tape."

Mr. Little and Uncle Pete started off toward the cellar.

"Tom — tell me about that tape recorder," said Uncle Nick.

"The tape is in a slot," said Tom. "We can't take that, can we?"

"Won't have time," Uncle Nick said. "What types of controls does it have?"

"A whole bunch," said Tom. "There's on and off, bass and treble, volume . . . "

"What makes the tape go ahead fast?"

asked Uncle Nick. "Can it do that?"

"Sure," said Tom. "They all have that. It's called 'fast-forward.'"

"I wonder," said Uncle Nick, "if we could send it ahead *past* where you got yourself recorded on the tape. Do we have time for that while Bigg is in the cellar putting the switch back on?"

"Sure," Tom said. "But won't Mr. Bigg notice it?"

"Maybe, maybe not," said Uncle Nick. "He may not realize it, especially if the people on the program are still talking about the same thing."

"Maybe it'll work," said Tom.

"Let's get into the living room," said Uncle Nick. "Get as close as we can, before the lights go out. We have to get up there fast, speed the tape forward as soon as the electricity comes on again, and get back down here before Bigg gets back from the cellar."

Tom took a deep breath. "I'm ready," he said.

"Lucy — you stay here with Mus Mus," said Uncle Nick.

"Aw!" said Lucy.

Uncle Nick and Tom went through the secret door into the Biggs' living room. Lucy held the door open a crack to watch.

"You see, Mus Mus," said Lucy to the white mouse, "just because Tom knows all about that dumb tape recorder, Uncle Nick takes him instead of me. It isn't fair!"

After a long wait, the voices on the tape recorder were still being heard. "In my opinion," one man said, "Lincoln's biggest mistake was..."

The sound stopped and the lights went out all over the house.

"George! What happened?" It was Mrs. Bigg from another room.

"Darn!" said George Bigg. "Blew a fuse right in the middle of that."

"I'll get some candles," said Mrs. Bigg.

"Where's the flashlight?" called Mr.

Bigg. "Ouch! Bumped my knee."

"Hanging by the cellar stairs," Mrs. Bigg answered.

Tom and Uncle Nick were busy climbing the electric cord to the tape recorder.

It was very dark on the shelf. Tom stumbled around trying to find the fast-forward button on the machine. "Here," he said finally, "I think this is it."

"Push it down, Tom," said Uncle Nick.

Tom grunted. "I'm trying to," he said. "It won't go."

"All together then," said Uncle Nick giving Tom a hand.

The two tiny people pushed.

"Come on, Tom — harder!" gasped Uncle Nick.

The lights came on and the button went down at almost the same time.

There was a whirring sound from the tape recorder.

"It's going," said Tom. "That's the tape reel going fast. How long should we let it go?"

"It'll have to be a guess," said Uncle Nick. "We'll stop when we hear Bigg on the cellar steps."

"I hear him already," Tom said.

"OK — stop it, Tom," said Uncle Nick.

"Oh golly!" Tom said.

"Stop it, Tom — let's get out of here!"

"I don't remember!" said Tom. "I forgot how!" The boy looked at all the buttons and levers and dials. He looked at the living room door. "He's coming!"

"Run for it!" whispered Uncle Nick. The two Littles slid down the electric cord. Mr. Bigg came in the room. The radiator with the secret door was too far away. Mr. Bigg might see them run for it. Uncle Nick and Tom hid behind a chair.

"What's going on around here?" shouted Mr. Bigg. "First the master switch is thrown — now the tape is running fast." He turned to the kitchen. "Did you fuss with this tape recorder?" he called to Mrs. Bigg.

"George Bigg — you know perfectly well I *never* touch that thing," said Mrs. Bigg.

"Well, something's cuckoo," said Mr. Bigg. "Oh well." He rewound the tape and located the place where someone was saying, "In my opinion, Lincoln's biggest mistake . . ."

"It's hopeless!" said Uncle Pete under the chair.

"I'll pull the plug," Tom said.

"He'd just put it back, Tom," said Uncle Nick. "We're trapped. And now he's going to find out about us. We've failed."

Just at that moment, a white mouse dashed across the floor right in front of Mr. Bigg.

"Mus Mus!" whispered Tom.

"A mouse!" yelled George Bigg.

The mouse ran to the far side of the room.

Mr. Bigg was out of his chair in a flash.

At the same time, Tom Little's voice came over the loudspeakers. "We interrupt this program. . ."

Mr. Bigg wasn't listening. "Hey, Alice!" he yelled. "There's a *white* mouse in the house. Where's the cat?"

Mrs. Bigg ran into the room.

"Get the cat!" yelled Mr. Bigg. He was on his knees looking under the furniture.

Tom's voice was warning about tiny people in the walls of houses, but the Biggs weren't listening. . . .

When it was all over, the Littles were back in their apartment. Mus Mus was safe in the passageway outside. Mrs. Bigg was setting mousetraps. And Mr. Bigg was napping in his chair.

The Littles sipped hot chocolate and talked over the Great Halloween Scare.

"Lucy saved us," said Mr. Little. He turned to his daughter. "Lucy — you're a hero!"

"I know," said Lucy. She smiled.

"Tell us how you did it, Lucy," said Uncle Pete. "How did you ever think of sending Mus Mus into the Biggs' living room?"

"It worked wonderfully," said Mr. Little. "It took their minds off the radio program."

"Yes, how did you think of it, Lucy?" asked Uncle Nick. "It was a brilliant plan."

Lucy looked around at everybody with a big grin on her face. "Well," she began, "first I . . ." Then she thought for a moment. "No, I decided to . . . *well* — I looked around and saw . . ." Finally, "Gee—somebody had to do *something*!" she said. "So I did!"

All the Littles laughed.

Their laughing woke up baby Betsy. And when she looked and saw all the happy faces, she laughed too.